Hutzinger

Published in the United States 2011 by
Blue Apple Books
515 Valley Street, Maplewood, NJ 07040
www.blueapplebooks.com
First Edition 09/11 Printed in Dongguan, China
ISBN: 978-1-60905-100-6

2 4 6 8 10 9 7 5 3

Bear in

LONG

Underwear

by Todd H. Doodler

🍎 BLUE APPLE BOOKS

Bear and his friends are inside drinking hot chocolate.

WHO'S GOT THE MARSHMALLOWS?

Bear is feeling cozy but a little cooped up
from being inside all day.
He looks out the window and says . . .

THE SNOW
HAS STOPPED
FALLING!

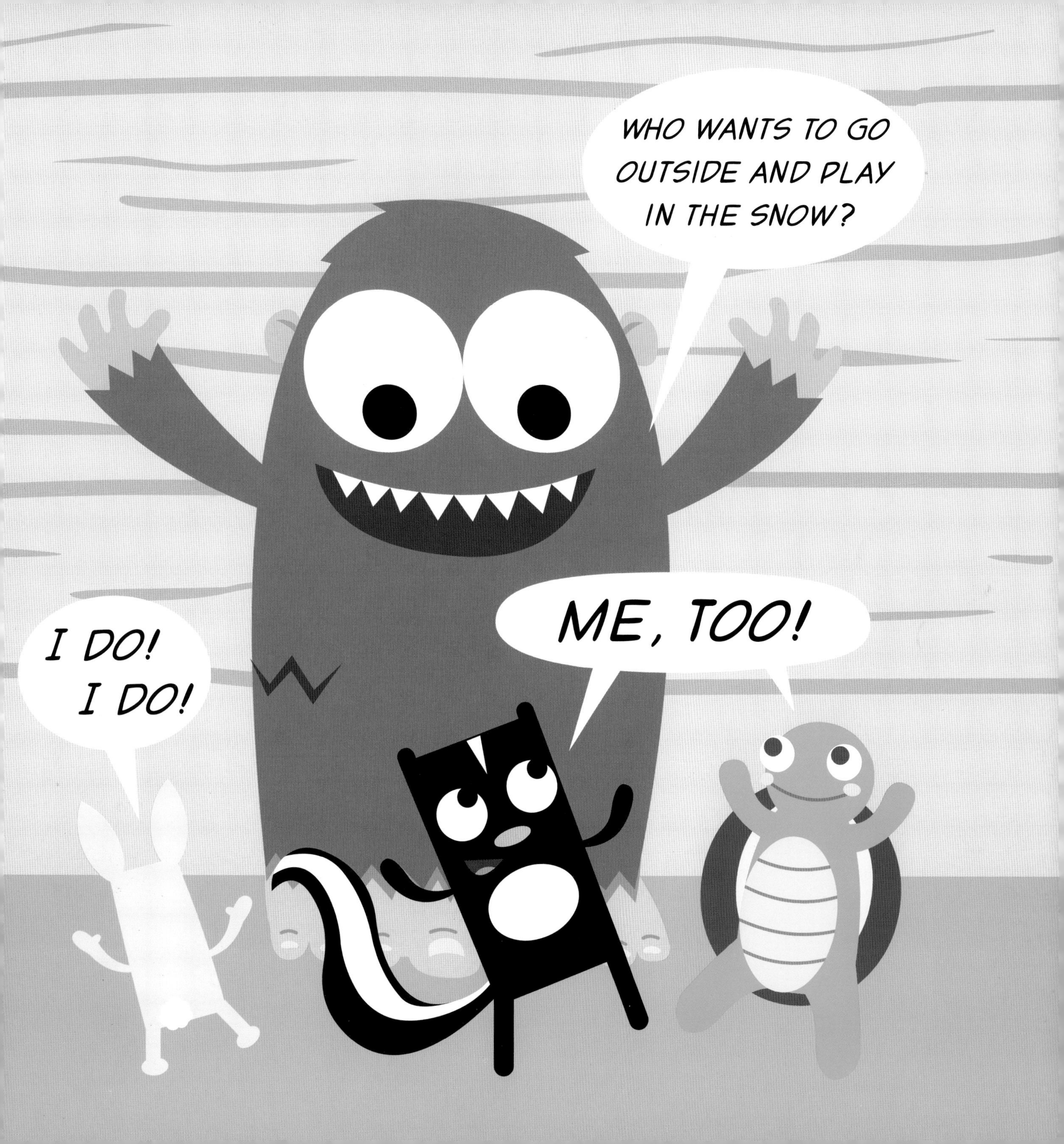
WHO WANTS TO GO OUTSIDE AND PLAY IN THE SNOW?
I DO! I DO!
ME, TOO!

scarves,

jackets,

and boots.

Everyone wants to do something different.

Rabbit and Skunk find sleds
and head for the top of the hill.

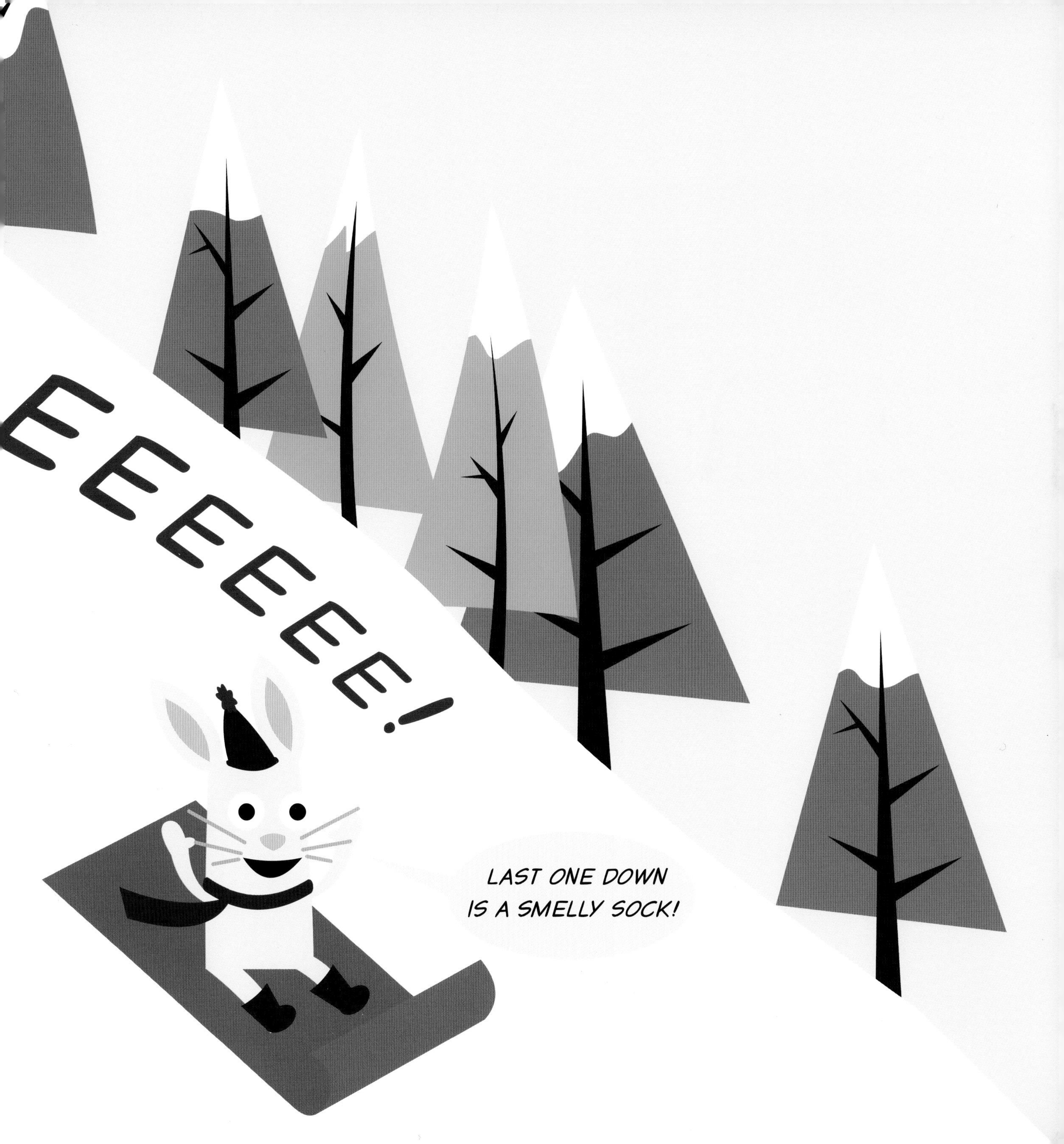
EEEEEEE!
LAST ONE DOWN
IS A SMELLY SOCK!

MINE'S PERFECT.

Beaver makes snow angels
with Cougar.

Then they catch snowflakes.

Turtle and Hedgy have a snowball fight.

Honey Bear and Deer join in the fun.

Bear decides
to build a
snowman.

Everyone has ideas for Bear.

Bear agrees. He puts his very own hat on the snowman.

Then he adds his scarf.

Bear puts his earmuffs,

his mittens,

and then his jacket on the snowman.

The snowman is dressed. But Bear is nearly bare!

Cougar asks Bear what he is wearing.

"This is my long underwear," Bear explains.
"I always wear this when it is cold and snowy."

Everyone wants underwear just like Bear!

Bear says, "There's lots more in the cabin."

Everyone picks a pair!

Look! Everyone has long underwear,
but there's one extra red pair.

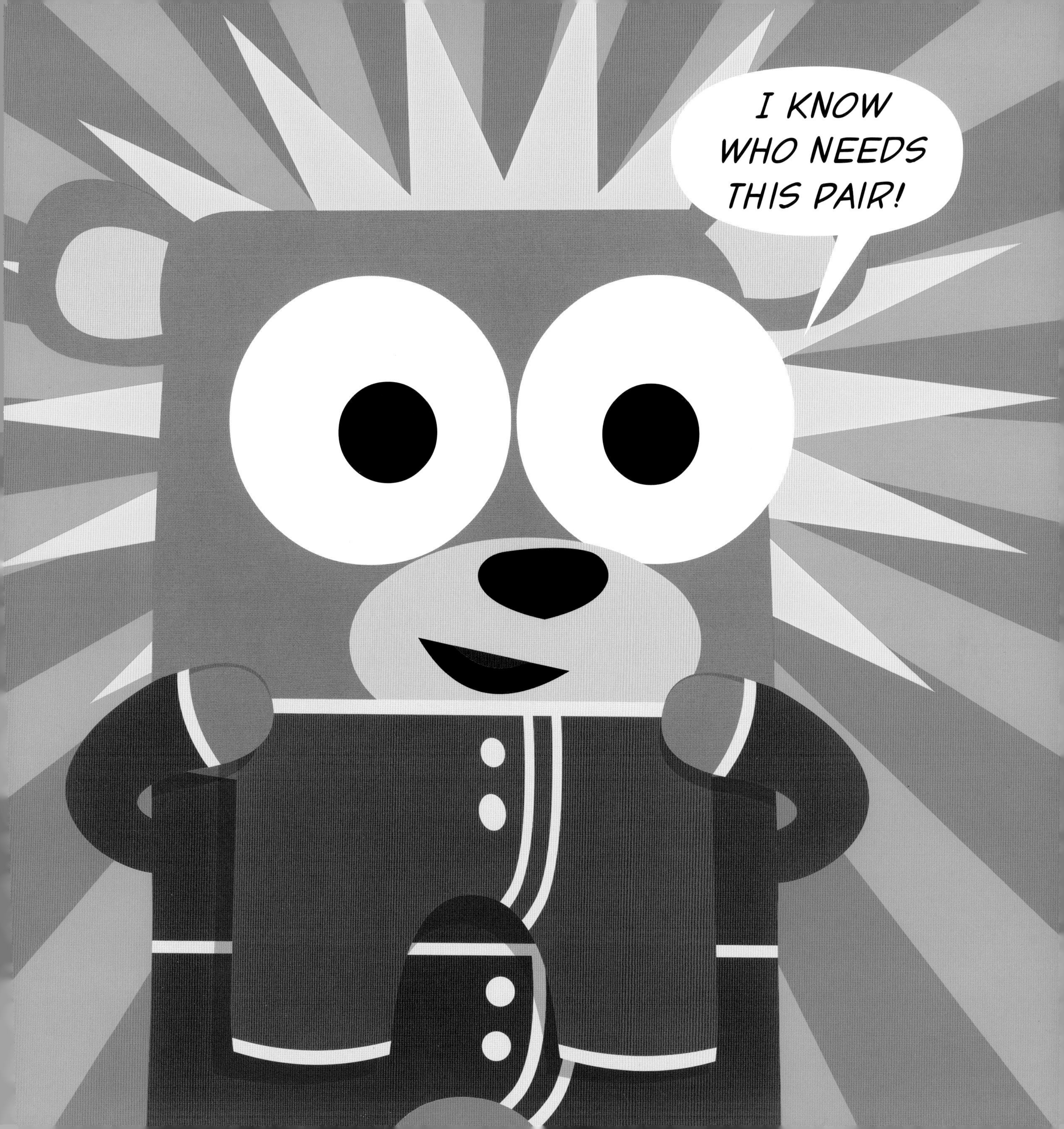
I KNOW WHO NEEDS THIS PAIR!

Snowman looks great in his long underwear!

It is the perfect winter pair!